The Jackdaw JinX

THE JACKDAW JINX

KATHY ASHFORD

Illustrated by Satoshi Kitamura

Andersen Press • London

For Josh, Joe, Jake and Isaac

This edition published in 2006 by
Andersen Press Limited,
20 Vauxhall Bridge Road, London SW1V 2SA
www.andersenpress.co.uk

Reprinted 2006, 2007

Text © Kathy Ashford, 2006
Illustrations © Satoshi Kitamura, 2006

The rights of Kathy Ashford and Satoshi Kitamura to be identified as
the author and illustrator of this work have been asserted by them in
accordance with the Copyright, Designs and Patents Act, 1988.

British Library Cataloguing in Publication Data available

ISBN 978 1 84270 540 7

Printed in the UK by CPI Bookmarque, Croydon, CR0 4TD

Chapter 1

'Get away from my ladder. Just clear off, before you cause an accident!' Mrs Bunion jabbed at me with her trowel.

'Never touched your ladder.'

'Don't you answer back, Robin Mills. I'll be speaking to your parents.'

'Nothing new there then.' No one calls me Robin and gets away with it. Rob's bad enough, Robin makes me cringe.

'I'm on to you, you know,' she screamed. 'Hanging around that filthy dump causing trouble. Sooner that place is built on the better. When I was your age I . . .'

And so on. If I was to make a list of my least favourite people in the world, Mrs Spiky Bunion would come top. There she is, day in and day out, up on that balcony spying on everyone and fussing over her manky cactuses. And what's with the red spotty glasses? She's like some demented owl with a skin rash. If I had a name like hers, last thing I'd do is wear glasses with buniony bumps all over them. Anyway, for the record, I never went

near her ladder. In fact I never go near any ladders if I can help it. Bad luck, aren't they? No, I was just walking along the pavement minding my own business when she started shrieking at me. She's always doing it, and if she's not shrieking at me, she's shrieking at someone else. All mean and sharp and cactussy. Mum reckons we should get her on that *Neighbours from Hell* programme. Sounds good to me, I'd do anything to get on TV.

With Mrs Bunion on the rampage, I thought I'd make myself scarce. So I went off up to 'that filthy dump', whistling very loudly all the way, just so she'd know where I was going. The dump, or the common as most people call it, is my second home, and a lot tidier than parts of my first home. Anyway, now they want to build offices on it. Which would be a big shame. Not for Mrs Bunion though, because the builders need to buy a bit of her garden to make room for the car park, so she'll be stinking rich. Filthy lucre, as Dad puts it.

The dump's full of useful things.

Really useful things, like bits of buggies and buckled bikes and broken baths. In fact, most of the stuff on my dump begins with 'b'. Maybe there's another dump in another town where people dump all the things beginning with 'c' like cracked cricket bats, crooked cartwheels and crushed cabbages. Now I come to think of it, Mrs Bunion begins with 'b'. Maybe she'll end up on my dump one day. Then I could turn her into something useful. Some hope.

Back to the plot. It's always like this on the dump, lots of unexpected things come along and you get side-

tracked. First job today was to check on Mum's 'Save our Dump' posters in case someone had ripped them down. There were three designs with different headlines spaced out along the railings. There was DON'T DUMP ON US, in bright red; GET DOWN IN THE DUMPS . . . SAVE OUR PARK, in turquoise; and WE'RE COMMON AND WE LIKE IT, in blue. They looked pretty cool. Just the odd crease here and there.

The next thing was to see what had arrived since I'd last been up. It was a bit disappointing to be honest. There was only one new thing – well, old thing actually – a rusty bike without a wheel. Still it could've been worse.

Sometimes you get a bike with no wheels, sometimes a bike with no wheels and no frame, and very very rarely a bike with no wheels, no handlebars and no frame. Which is really no bike at all. It's the same with buckets. Sometimes you find a bucket with no hole, a *whole* bucket, and sometimes a bucket with a hole so big that there's more hole than bucket. Then what have you found, a bucket or a hole?

I checked the bike over and stood it up against the hedge. Someone had been digging near the bushes, it was probably because of the new offices. There was a deep trench with fresh earth piled high on one side. I didn't like to think of strangers poking around on my dump. I was just climbing over some rusty bedsprings to reach the old bath when I heard a strange croaking sound.

'Jrrrrrrk Jrrrrrk.' Loud and echoey.

'Jrrrrrrk Jrrrrrk.'

It was a bit spooky to be honest.

'Jrrrrrrk Jrrrrrk.' The sound was really close this time. Perhaps it was a frog. I edged forward. Everest would be a cinch compared to climbing over other people's slippery rubbish. As I stooped down beside the bath, I saw a scrawny black creature, all claws and beak. It was a bird – you don't get duck-billed platypuses in England, not even on my dump – and it was the weirdest-looking thing. The ugly duckling had nothing on it. Although it was still a baby it was already the size of a blackbird, with a very bald head. The feathers on the rest of its body were ragged and its pale eyes looked, well, cross. Very cross indeed. When it saw me it glared and fluttered sideways.

'Jrrrrrrk Jrrrrrk.'
'What are you?' I said.
'JRRRRRRR-
RRRRRRK,' it screeched
and puffed its feathers up.
Was it trying to say 'rook', or
was it calling me a 'jerk'. I
couldn't decide.
I didn't want to pick it up,
partly because I didn't like
the look of its great black beak, but
also because I was worried about its
parents. I once read a story about a
man being mobbed by crows because
he'd picked up a baby bird that had
fallen from a tree. The parents were
protecting it. The man was pecked so
hard he had to be taken to hospital.
What if this was a crow? Just my luck.

Trouble was that if it stayed in the
shade against the bath its mum and
dad might never see it, and then it
would probably be eaten by

something. There were loads of foxes on the dump, you could tell that from the smell. I decided it was best to shoo it away from the bath onto a pile of rubble and then, if its parents were searching for it, they'd easily spot it from the trees. But shooing it wasn't easy. I waved my hands in the air like a manic scarecrow and stamped my feet.

It stood its ground.

'Go on! Budge!' I shouted.

It looked a bit surprised.

Maybe it thought 'budge' was short for budgerigar.

'Look, just move, OK? Scram. Mum and Dad . . . in trees. Missing you.'

It stayed very still. Too still. It watched my arms whirling around and then slowly, very slowly, began to close its eyes. First one eye blinked, then the other, then they shut altogether. What was the matter with the thing? There I was stamping about and whooshing and what did it do? Fall asleep that's what. Hypnotised by my seesawing arms. Stupid creature, it wouldn't last five minutes if it dropped off as easily as that.

I looked up into the trees, but there was no sign of any anxious-looking parents. Didn't they mind their son – or daughter – talking to strangers? Maybe they'd read the writing on the wall, or, in this case, seen the posters, and decided to get out before the dump was flattened. There was nothing else for it, I would have to take it home. It didn't look nearly as fierce with its eyes shut.

I reached out and put both hands round its body. Its feathers were puffed up in sleep, but underneath it felt scrawny and thin. And, yes, it was as light as a feather. It hardly seemed

to notice what I was doing. One eye
half opened and flicked shut, the
eyelids were the colour of quick
moulding clay and ridged like a
ploughed field.

I tucked the baby bird carefully
inside my fleece. At first its claws
rested on the palm of my right hand,
then they tightened around my fingers.
They scratched a bit. Not as sharp as
the claws on our cats though. It was a
nice feeling, and I couldn't help
thinking that the dump had given me
its greatest treasure yet. And, of
course, it began with a 'b'. Who

knows, if it was a rare bird, they'd have to save the dump as a special nesting area. But treasures from the dump didn't always turn out like you thought they would.

And this bird was no different.

Chapter 2

'You can't keep him you know,' said
Mole.

Mole and I were sitting on the
kitchen floor at my house watching Joe
watching us from an empty Kleenex
box. You see things had moved on
slightly since the last chapter. First of
all, I'd decided to call the bird Joe. It
was because of my Gran. She was the
bird person in our family. As far back
as I can remember, she'd kept budgies.
They were always yellow and they
were always called Joe, or sometimes

Joey if she was in a particularly good mood. Whenever one of them died, we'd get her another straight away and she'd hardly notice any difference. So my bird had to be Joe too. Better Joe than Robin.

And what about Mole? Mole isn't an animal, she's a person. She's a bit like a real mole in some ways, although that's not how she got her name. Mole has lots of smooth black hair and dark eyes. She's rather small and pale and a bit shy. She lives next door and we've known each other for years and years and years. So the first thing I did when I got home with Joe was to call Mole and tell her to get round to my house

quick. Then I emptied some of the
Kleenex out of the box and fluffed the
rest up a bit to make a comfortable
place for Joe and put him inside. He
was still very sleepy. Maybe he was in
shock or something. I was just

wondering whether I should make him a cup of very sweet tea to perk him up when Mole came in. I told her what had happened and she just stared at Joe in the Kleenex box and that's when she said, 'You can't keep him, you know.'

'Why not?' I said.

'Because he's wild and he belongs in the woods. He needs his mum and dad. He'll die.'

'He would've died if I'd left him to the foxes. His parents weren't around.'

I was feeling a bit miffed to be honest. I was pretty sure my mum and dad would kick up a fuss about Joe, but I'd at least thought that Mole would be on my side. We always backed each other up. Like the time we faked notes to get out of the class detention. We were a team.

'Jackdaws like to live in flocks. They need company,' said Mole.

'Jackdaws? How d'you know it's a jackdaw?'

'It's the eyes. See how pale they are? And the beak. Smaller than a rook's.'

She pointed at Joe; he winked a pale blue eye at her.

'You sure?'

'*Sure I'm sure,*' said Mole in her best American accent. 'Here, give him this old sock, it'll make him more comfortable.' She pulled a shapeless green woolly thing from her pocket. Mole always has the oddest things in her pockets. This was a sock, an odd sock.

'Thanks,' I said. *Joe Jackdaw?* 'That sounds great.' Good old Mole. It was no surprise that she knew all about Joe. Her family were experts on nature, always putting splints on lizards' legs, cutting up bacon for tadpoles or feeding badgers toast and marmalade.

'So are jackdaws rare?' I said. 'Cause they couldn't shut the dump if it was a nesting place for rare birds.'

'See that pigeon through the window?' said Mole. 'About as rare as that.'

'Oh.' That was a shame. Even I knew pigeons weren't rare. I'd been to Trafalgar Square. Well, he might not save the dump, but I still wanted to keep him. 'Honestly, Mole, his parents weren't around. And he's not a baby anymore. He can't fly very well, but he can flutter a few feet, so he would've been leaving home soon anyway. We could both look after him.'

'You can't put him in a cage. It wouldn't be fair.'

'Course not.'

'And jackdaws aren't exactly the easiest birds to keep. They can be a bit strange. I'm not sure you should risk it.' Talk about patronising – just 'cos she knew more about animals than me. Still, I didn't like the bit about *risk*.

'What d'you mean?' I said.

'There are lots of stories about them. Good omens, bad omens. Or should I say bird omens. And let's face it, you're already obsessed with all that stuff – walking round ladders, stepping in the squares, touching wood every five minutes. You'll never cope with a jackdaw jinx.'

'What sort of jinx?' I said, crossing my fingers behind my back. Was this just a wind-up or was she trying to tell me something serious. 'I know jackdaws are s'posed to like shiny things but that's not necessarily bad. That could be good. I like collecting stuff too, from the dump. Birds of a feather, me and Joe.'

'Well try this for starters,' said Mole. 'A single jackdaw perched on a roof means bad luck for the family.'

'Well Joe's not on a roof, is he?' I said cautiously. 'He's in a Kleenex box.'

'Yeah, well he won't be in a Kleenex box forever will he? He'll soon be flying around and then you'll be in trouble. And so will everyone in the street since he's bound to fly from roof to roof. What if the whole street gets hit by a plague of locusts or something? Or a meteorite?' She put on her news reporter voice. *'Not since the dinosaurs has such wholesale destruction been seen, all the inhabitants of Win Hill wiped out at a single stroke.'*

'How can a jackdaw sitting on a roof possibly be bad luck? They must perch on roofs all the time.'

'OK,' said Mole, 'How about this? A *flock* of jackdaws on your house is s'posed to mean you'll get loads of money. Win the Lottery or something. Maybe we could persuade him to bring his friends round. *A lottery syndicate of neighbours from Win Hill today won the largest rollover jackpot of all time. Said Robin Mills, resident at Number 114, "We owe it all to a flock of jackdaws."'*

'Shut up! I'm not Robin. Winning a fortune is just fine by me. Is that it?'

'Nearly. Flocks of jackdaws swooping around mean—'

'West Ham's going to win the FA cup?' I suggested.

'No. A terrible storm.'

'Silly me. Flocks of pigs flying around mean West Ham's going to win the FA cup. Honestly Mole, swooping jackdaws don't prove anything. It's like saying cows lying down mean rain. Cows don't cause rain by lying down, they just lie down 'cos they know it's going to rain and they want to keep a dry patch. Must be the same with jackdaws and storms. It's not a proper jinx. If that's the worst, I'll definitely be keeping him.'

'Fine,' said Mole. 'Keep him. It's best you don't know the other stuff.'

'What other stuff?'

'I'm not telling you. It's too creepy.' I could tell she was really enjoying this.

'Oh come off it, Mole, you have to tell me now. What is it? *On the stroke of midnight, jackdaws transform into vampire bats and suck the blood of the nearest living thing?* He looks likely to do that, doesn't he?'

Mole and I looked down at Joe winking in the Kleenex box. We'd got so involved we'd almost forgotten he was there.

'All right. Here goes,' said Mole. 'If a jackdaw flies down a chimney it means death in the household.'

Call me pathetic, but the moment she said it, a shiver ran down my spine and goosebumps rose up on my arms.

I tried to put a brave face on it. 'Well, it would mean death wouldn't it, if the fire was lit?'

'No, not death to the jackdaw. Death to someone in the house . . .'

'Oh.' I felt as if I'd just been punched in the stomach. 'Are you sure?'

''Course I'm not sure, they're just stories. Probably a load of rubbish. Anyway, if you're worried, you could always put a grating in to block the chimney. We've got one of those.'

Typical Mole, one minute she's scaring you stupid, the next she's offering you roofing tips. 'You're not gonna let a few silly stories change your mind about Joe are you?' she said.

'Maybe we should take him back,' I said slowly. It was easy for Mole to be cool about all this, she didn't have a Gran who stayed in bed all day whenever Friday 13th came round.

'His parents will've given up on him

by now,' said Mole. 'You're not going to abandon him too, are you? I'm sure he'll be OK. Touch wood!'

'That's settled then. I'm keeping him.'

Chapter 3

The trouble with Mole is, she's not
bothered by the things that worry
most people – like death and
destruction. She sees life differently.
Take how she got her name. When she
was about five, she was playing on the
edge of the dump when she found a
dead mole. It still looked perfect to
her, all dark and velvety with large
hands almost like ours. Now most of
us would have had a good look and
run on, or maybe we'd've poked it
with a stick or something. But Mole

thought it was really cool. It didn't matter that it was dead. And she couldn't stand the idea of it lying outside and getting eaten by a fox or something. Bit like me with Joe Jackdaw. So she picked it up and carried it home. That evening she took it to bed with her and for the next five nights it lay on her pillow until her mum decided it was beginning to smell and they gave it a proper burial in the garden. And after that everyone stopped calling her Rosie and called her Mole. And you've got to respect a girl who sleeps with a dead mole, haven't you? Either that or have her put away.

Anyway, right now, Mole's jackdaw jinx wasn't my biggest problem. Joe wouldn't be staying around long enough to fly down anyone's chimney unless I could square it with my mum and dad. After Mole had gone home, I moved the plates and dishes off the shelf near the boiler and put Joe's box up there. It was a great place for him. Nice and warm, a few easy hops to the floor and pretty impossible to reach for our two cats. There was a window up high which could be propped open so that when Joe got a bit bigger he would be able to fly in and out whenever he wanted. For the time being the kitchen was going to be his base. I sat down and took him onto the palm of my hand and waited for Mum and Dad. He was looking so calm and peaceful, how could they resist him?

But Joe wasn't about to make life easy for me. As soon as I sat down, his eyes shot open and he fluttered from my hands onto the floor, leaving a large grey splurt on the rug. Then he hopped over to the cat's meat and pecked at it a few times. Are jackdaws carnivores or vegetarians? Maybe they are omnivores like humans. Anyway the cat's food was going down better

than the warm milk I'd given him earlier. I took a piece of bread and crumbled it onto the floor.

'Joe,' I called, 'over here, tea's up.'

The noise startled him. Flicking the cat's dish over with one wing, he launched himself erratically into the air and onto the nearest shelf. A neat pile of cups and saucers crashed to the floor, sending him into a bigger spin. He flew at the window, hit it with a nasty thump and fell back into the sink, shattering a couple of glasses as he went.

'What's going on?' screamed Mum standing in the doorway. 'What on earth is that thing doing in here?'

Panicking, Joe rocketed straight for her. His claws sank into the top of her head and he deposited another large splurt right on her fringe. Things were not going to plan. Mum's eyes stared wildly as the grey blob ran slowly down the ridge of her nose.

'Stay still, Mum, I'll get him off you. He won't hurt you. You shouldn't have scared him.'

'*Me, scare him?* A vulture dive-bombs me in my kitchen because *I've* scared *him.* Do me a favour!'

'It's not a vulture, it's a jackdaw,' I said, grabbing Joe firmly and pulling

him off her head – some of her hair was tangled in his claws.

'I don't care if it's Posh Spice, I want that thing out of here by the time I get back from the bathroom.' Posh Spice? No one calls her that anymore.

It was a shame Mum and Joe got off to such a bad start. I s'pose you couldn't really blame her for feeling miffed, what with that grey blob trickling down her face. I wouldn't've been too happy myself.

'Come on, Joe, you're going to have to do better than that.'

I put him back in his box. If he would just drop off to sleep again before she came back down we could start all over again. Then I had an idea. I began slowly seesawing my arms around, just like I did on the dump. Joe looked startled at first, but then slowly and surely the blinking started and he went straight off to sleep. With perfect timing, Dad walked in. It was my lucky day, he was on his mobile talking to someone from work.

'Hi, Rob, good day?' he mouthed, pointing to the phone to show he was in the middle of a conversation.

'Great, Dad. Look what I've found. It's a jackdaw, I saved its life and it's come to live with us.'

'Fine, sounds good,' said Dad, holding his hand over the mouthpiece. 'Can't talk now, it's Craig from the office.'

That's the good thing about Dad, he'll always ask you questions when he's on his mobile but he never listens to the answers. I could've told him I'd sold the house to Mrs

Bunion and he'd still have said, 'Fine, sounds good.'

So that was Dad sorted. My older sister Becky shouldn't be a problem either, she was hardly ever at home and wasn't likely to notice Joe unless he stood between her and the mirror. So the only issue was Mum. Fresh from washing her hair, she was in the lounge working on some more 'Save the Dump' posters. To be honest I don't think Mum's really cut out for a career in advertising but she was dead set on stopping those offices and was coming up with several new posters each day. She was just putting the finishing touches to BE A DUMP-LING, JOIN OUR CAMPAIGN, when I walked in carrying Joe in his Kleenex box. He was fast asleep.

'I didn't know you wanted another pet,' said Mum. 'Aren't the two cats enough? Couldn't you have settled for a hamster or something?'

'He's not really a pet. He's free to go.'

'Where did you find him?' She peered in at Joe.

'On the dump. There must be loads of birds nesting up there.'

'Oh, I see.' This was something in Joe's favour. As far as Mum was concerned, nothing bad could possibly come out of the dump. 'OK, we'll give it a try. Just for a few days. But, Rob, if anything, anything at all, goes wrong again, he's out. Got it?'

'What could go wrong?' I said, failing to mention the small matter of bad luck, storms and death in the household.

Chapter 4

Living with Joe wasn't exactly a piece
of cake. The only other pets that had
really been 'mine' were a couple of
woodlice in a match box and even the
wildest woodlouse couldn't cause as
much trouble as a jackdaw. Don't get
me wrong. He was great to have
around and as he soared down onto
my wrist in the street I felt really
proud, like some sort of medieval
knight with a falcon. Joe could also be
incredibly gentle, preening my hair,
running his beak slowly through each

strand, spiking it up better than any
gel. And when there was trouble, Joe
was always on our side, like the time
he dive-bombed Slick Nick for
running off with Mole's
mobile phone.

But there is a
downside to living
with a wild bird.
The mess for
starters.
Within a few
days there were
grey splurts all
over the house,
in the pages of
our favourite books, across the kitchen
table and, worse still, inside the
computer keyboard. Take a look at the
instructions that go with your
computer and I guarantee you'll find
nothing useful about how to clean
sloppy bird droppings out of the

workings. The unmistakeable cry of, 'Splurt Alert', could be heard every hour or so around the house. And guess who was supposed to jump to it? I always seemed to be rushing around with a dishcloth, or maybe a tooth brush to get into those places dishcloths just don't reach. The trick was never to use the wrong toothbrush for doing your teeth.

Now you might have thought that Mole would have helped me out on this. After all, Joe was nearly as much her jackdaw as mine, but no, 'Splurt Alert' seemed to act as a signal for her to make herself scarce.

'Told you it wasn't easy owning a jackdaw,' she said one day as I was wiping the TV screen for the third time in ten minutes.

'It's pretty obvious why some people think jackdaws are bad luck,' I said gloomily. 'Still, it seems it's only bad

luck for me. I'm the one with the dishcloth, after all.'

'Let's hope that's all it means,' said Mole darkly. But she couldn't wind me up with the jackdaw jinx stuff anymore. By this time Joe was just part of normal life, like wet Sundays or scuffed shoes.

Joe didn't just cause mess, he went in for what Mum described as 'deliberate wholesale destruction'. He totally mangled the poor wooden cuckoo that came out of the clock every half hour. He would wait for it to appear and then go for it, pecking and slicing with his beak. After a week or two the cuckoo would come

out with this petrified look on its face
and leap back in as quickly as possible
slamming the door behind it. Mole
said Joe was wreaking revenge on real
cuckoos for taking over other birds'
nests.

Then there was Joe's regular game of
skittles. This was normally reserved for
Sunday evenings when we were all
snoozing in front of the TV. He would
walk slowly along Mum's row of
special coffee pots knocking the lids
off alternately. Tip one, leave one, tip
one, leave one. Pretty clever, eh? Never
two pots in a row. And each time he'd
look at us waiting for a reaction. The
first time he did it, we all leapt to our

feet screaming and waving and this gave him the excuse to take off in a great hurry causing the pots to fly in all directions. The trick was to sit tight and let him get on with it. Fewer breakages that way.

The damage didn't stop with the pots and pans. Joe was obsessed with Becky's earrings. She would insist on wearing, not just one, but a row of shiny studs on each lobe which of course he *had* to have. And the fuss she made just because she got pecked a few times. Becky's boyfriend, Mick, didn't come off much better either. Mick suffered from acne, and this summer he had an enormous spot in the middle of his forehead. As far as Joe was concerned, that beautiful shiny spot had to go. He'd sit on Mick's shoulder preening Mick's hair to lull him into a false sense of security and then *ouch!* He'd have a go at that pimple. Then, regular as clockwork, Dad would say, 'Oh dear, Mick, having a *spot* of bother with Joe, are you?' Becky just looked daggers.

There was another spot of bother over table manners. When it came to food, what Joe enjoyed most was sharing. At mealtimes he would wander backwards and forwards between our plates taking a bit of mashed potato here, a couple of peas there. I know it sounds disgusting, but after a few weeks everyone in our family had more or less got used to it. Everyone except Gran.

Although Gran was supposed to be a bird lover, she didn't approve of Joe at all. As far as she was concerned, birds should be kept in cages and only allowed out on special occasions. And as for his being on the table at dinner times, well that was unthinkable. She'd spent years training us at the dinner table, telling us to eat with our elbows shut, keep our mouths in and all that stuff. And here was Joe breaking all her sacred rules one by one.

One particular lunchtime, Gran had just sat down when Joe flew in through the window and landed on the table. He saw the mashed potato and hopped straight over to Gran's plate.

'Ugh! Get that thing off the table.' Gran waved her napkin at Joe.

'But Gran, he always goes on the—' I began.

'Yes, get him off, Rob,' said Mum. 'You know he's not allowed on the table.'

'Mum?!' I said in disbelief, but one look at her face made me keep quiet. 'Err, I'll catch him.'

Joe wasn't going to give himself up that easily. Quite the opposite. He hopped onto the edge of Gran's plate, took a mouthful of her potato and did

his beak shaking trick, speckling her glasses with mash. This was war. With a howl of rage, Gran picked her knitting needles from her lap and thrashed around at Joe. It was a great game, the more she thrashed about, the more Joe ducked and dodged, darting at her plate to grab another slurp of mash.

'Do something!' shrieked Gran.

'We're trying,' said Mum. 'He thinks you're trying to stop him getting his dinner.'

'*His* dinner?! It's disgusting. I'll not stay here another minute. This house is like a wretched zoo. It'll all end in tears. You mark my words.'

She stood up, gave us her prophet-of-doom glare and turned on her heel. As she stomped out of the room, he flew above her letting go a string of grey splurts as he went. It was like watching a warplane releasing bombs

over enemy territory. Fortunately for Gran, and probably for Joe too, none of them hit.

It was a long time before Gran had dinner at our house again. And by that time Joe had gained a much more sinister enemy. Spiky Bunion.

Remember her? The cactus lady with the spotty glasses. She'd had it in for Joe from the start and it was down to Mrs Bunion that the first of Mole's jackdaw omens came true.

Chapter 5

I swear that Joe had only been with us about two minutes when Mrs Bunion started complaining about him.

'She's switched on her fun detector and fixed it on Joe,' said Mole. *'The Bunion patent fun detector designed to seek out and destroy all happiness known to man.'*

It had been the same when we got our satellite dish. Mrs Bunion couldn't possibly have seen it because it was round the back of the house. But she still claimed the satellite signals were giving her cactuses 'droop'. Whatever that may be. And of course Joe could cause more problems than a hundred satellite dishes.

It all began with the 'unpleasant deposits' which Joe left on her plants.

Mole tried pointing out to Mrs Bunion that people pay a lot of money for bird poo in some parts of the world and she could collect it for sale or use it as fertiliser. But Mrs Bunion wasn't going to be palmed off that easily.

'Criminal damage, I call it. And he's pecking at the stems. I tell you, either you pay for the damage, or I'll be on to the police. In my day, pests like that would have been shot.'

'And children would've been sent up chimneys,' muttered Mole.

'It's not Joe that needs shooting,' I said as Mrs Bunion went off down the path. 'We'll just have to keep him away

from her as much as we can.' But this
was going to be tough. Trouble was,
Joe and Mrs Bunion had more in
common than you might have thought
– neither of them could keep their
beaks out of other people's business.

It was about three months after Joe
arrived that the Mrs Bunion problem
got out of hand. The summer holidays
had just begun and Mole and I were
standing outside our houses looking
for the Emerald. The Emerald was a
piece of stripy green glass about the
size of a twopence piece. It blended in
with the patchy concrete, stones and
gravel that made up the road outside
our houses. There was no tarmac at
the top of Win Hill, that fizzled out
about halfway up where the posh
houses ended.

Mole and I must have spent about
a quarter of our lives looking for the
Emerald. When we were little we used

to race to be the first to find it and
even now I'd get a kick if I spotted it
before Mole. Of course we knew it
wasn't a real emerald, but I always felt
it had some sort of special power. Not
that it was magical. It couldn't turn
people into cabbages or anything,
otherwise we'd've used it on
Mrs Bunion ages ago. No, the odd
thing about the Emerald was just that
it was so hard to find. It didn't matter
that you'd had your foot on it five
minutes before, if you turned away
and tried to come back to it, it had
always gone. Even marking the spot
didn't help. One night I drew a chalk
line around it so I'd be sure to be the
first to find it the next day. But when I
came back the Emerald wasn't inside
the line, it was about a metre outside.
How d'you explain that? It must have
escaped in the night. Of course I
couldn't tell Mole, that would have

meant admitting I'd been cheating.

This particular day we'd decided to train Joe to find the Emerald. I don't know why we hadn't tried it before. People say jackdaws can do anything. And Joe obviously had nothing planned for the morning. He was standing in the middle of the road, wings outstretched, head on one side, doing a spot of sunbathing. The feathers on his neck and under his wings were all damp and sweaty and he smelt really strongly of bird tables. Well, I suppose he smelt of birds really and bird tables smell of birds too. If you've got a bird table, go and smell it now and you'll see what I mean. I'll put the story on pause for a moment 'til you get back. Anyway, right now all Joe needed was a pair of sunglasses and a long cold drink and he'd've looked perfect on a brochure advertising beach holidays.

'Come on, Joe, wake up,' I said, poking him in the ribs. 'You can help us find the Emerald.'

'It's round here somewhere,' said Mole. 'I'm sure I caught sight of it just now. Find!'

'How can he find it if we can't even show him what he's s'posed to find?'

'Ouch!' said Mole. 'He nipped my ear.'

'That's 'cos he wants us to get on with it. Things to do, places to go, birds to meet, he can't hang around here all day.'

'Come on,' said Mole, for about the thousandth time, 'if we start by Mrs Bunion's gate and walk diagonally towards your gate we should pass the Emerald in the middle.'

'Bother, he's gone.' We watched helplessly as Joe flew straight over to Mrs Bunion's house and in through the top window. 'Birdbrain! We're for it now. Why does he always have to go where he's not wanted?'

'We'll have to get him out,' said Mole. 'Mrs Bunion was complaining to the Broomfields about him yesterday. Said he was the neighbourhood nuisance and that he was even *worse than those brats*. S'pose she meant us.'

'I know,' I said. 'She threatened my dad with the pest control people again.'

'Your dad's not that much of a pest is he?'

'No but Joe is.'

'Oh. What if she puts down poison pellets or something? Come on, let's go and get him.'

'How? And where's Mrs Bunion?' I peered through the hedge. As usual her front window was covered with thick blinds. 'I'm not going near that house if she's around.'

'Let's whistle,' said Mole. We'd been teaching Joe to come to a special signal. It hadn't worked very well so far, but it was worth a go. I put my fingers to my lips and blew as hard as I could. We didn't get Joe, but we did get Mrs Bunion. A very red-faced Mrs Bunion glaring ferociously through her buniony frames and mouthing things at us.

'She's either telling us to *clear* off,' I said, 'or something ruder.'

'She's disappeared,' said Mole. 'She must be coming to the door. Retreat!' Mole and I ran back to my garden. As we looked back across we saw Joe fly out of Mrs Bunion's window and onto her roof. He seemed to have something in his beak. He stayed up there for a few minutes, sauntering around as if he owned the place.

'Bad luck for Mrs B, then,' grinned Mole. 'One lonely jackdaw on the roof.'

'It'll be bad luck for Joe if she sees him. Doesn't he know he's in mortal danger?'

I tried another whistle. This time, it seemed to work. Joe came swooping down and landed in the middle of the road. He began sharpening his beak on the concrete.

'Wow! Look what he's found,' said Mole, bending over Joe. 'The Emerald.'

Chapter 6

That night we were all slumped in front of the TV watching *The Bill* – it's a police soap and we're addicted to it. We'd just got to a scary point in the plot when there was a loud ring on our door bell. My heart sank. It had to be Mrs Bunion, she must have discovered that Joe had been inside her house. Becky went to answer the door and came back in with a policeman! We all jumped to our feet. One minute the police were on the TV, the next they were in our living room. How did they manage that?

But this was the real McCoy, as Dad would say. The policeman was about eight foot tall and six foot wide, though I think that was mainly the padded jacket. He had a radio that spluttered all the time and a cap. No helmet. Policemen in cars don't wear helmets because they would fall off when they get in and out. Big Ears didn't have this problem because he had a convertible.

'Mr and Mrs Mills?' he said, getting his notebook out. 'There've been a couple of burglaries in the neighbourhood. Just came round to check if you'd seen anything.'

'Burglaries?' gasped Mum. She sounded really shocked. Maybe the policeman thought she sounded too shocked. Or maybe she was showing just the right amount of shockedness to get herself crossed off his list of

suspects.

'Yes, one of them was right opposite. Mrs Bunyan's house.'

'Bunion?' I said.

'Yes, know Mrs Bunyan do you?' The policeman turned a rather suspicious-looking eye on me. And of course I blushed. Well you would, wouldn't you?

'Of course he knows her, officer, we all do . . . unfortunately,' said Dad. Really he could be quite on the ball when he wasn't on his mobile.

'*Never seen her before in my life.*' This wasn't one of us, this was *The Bill*, still blaring away in the corner of the room.

'Would you mind turning the television off?' said the officer. I wanted to ask him why. Was it because he was recording it to watch later and didn't want to know what had happened?

'*That's enough of your cheek,*' said an

officer on the screen as Dad flicked the switch.

'What's been going on?' said Dad. 'I saw Mrs Bunyan this morning and she didn't say anything. Not about that anyway. 'Course she had plenty of other things to say.'

'It only happened this afternoon,' said the policeman.

'What did they take?' said Becky.

'And how did they get in?' said Mum. You could tell we'd been watching *The Bill*, we were asking all the right questions. 'I didn't know we had a problem with burglars round here,' Mum continued. 'Must admit we always leave our windows open.'

'Well, I strongly advise you to lock them,' said the policeman. 'Least 'til we've got this sorted out. Mind you, in both cases it happened while there was someone in the house. We think the thieves got in through an upstairs window. Not so difficult in Mrs Bunyan's case since there was a ladder leaning up against the wall.'

'There always is,' said Dad. 'It's how she gets onto her cactus balcony.'

'What did they take?' said Becky again. I had wanted to ask this myself, but I was starting to get an iffy feeling inside, like you do when you've eaten just that one too many chocolate muffins.

'Not a lot, as it happens. A few pieces of jewellery. Odd really, because they left some cash behind. And at the Whites' house three doors down, they didn't even bother to take the laptop. So did any of you notice anything strange this afternoon? Anything at all?'

'No,' said Mum.

'There's been quite a little crimewave round here,' continued the policeman. 'We're putting these latest incidents together with another last week when someone reported a watch chain missing. They couldn't be sure it had been stolen, but now it looks like we've got three crimes. Don't s'pose you're missing anything are you? Bits of jewellery or anything?'

'No,' I said, rather too loudly judging from the way everyone turned to look at me. 'At least Mum said the milk money disappeared one day. That's all.'

'Ah, you must be the one seen loitering near Mrs Bunyan's house. Sure you didn't see anything, young man?' The policeman gave me one of those searching looks. They do that a lot on *The Bill* too. 'Mrs Bunyan said she saw you with, er, Brown Mole?'

'Not quite,' laughed Mum. 'He must've been with Mole Black. She's the girl next door. Did you notice anything, Rob?'

'No,' I said. 'We were just looking for the Emerald like we always do.'

'The emerald?' said the policeman. 'So you are missing some jewellery?'

'It's just a bit of old glass,' said Mum.

'Anyway,' I continued, 'Mrs Bunion started shouting at us for no reason.'

'Nothing new there then,' said Dad.

'Well, we'll leave it at that for now,' said the policeman. 'Just make sure you've not lost anything and keep your eyes peeled.' And he went.

'I'm off upstairs,' said Becky, 'I need to check none of my earrings are missing.'

'Er, where's Joe?' I said.

'Haven't seen him all evening,' said Mum.

'I'd better go round to Mole's house and see if he's there,' I said.

'Yes, maybe we should keep a close eye on him,' said Mum, 'We don't want him getting mixed up with a burglar.'

'Heaven forbid.' I slipped out. I was

beginning to think Mum had been right and I should've settled for a hamster after all.

Chapter 7

'We've got to talk,' I said as Mole opened the door. 'It's urgent.'

'You look as if you've seen a ghost,' said Mole.

'Not a ghost, a burglar.'

'What?'

'A burglar, and he's sitting on your wrist.'

Mole stared at Joe. Joe put his head on one side and stared at his feet.

He fluffed his feathers up and looked embarrassed. Embarrassed and smug at the same time. Like you would if someone said you were the best footballer the school's ever had. Not that it's ever happened to me.

'You might get cat burglars, but you don't get bird ones,' said Mole. Then added thoughtfully, 'You don't, Joe, do you?'

Joe tried to look modest.

'There's been a burglary at Mrs Bunion's this afternoon, and another down the road. They got in through an upstairs window and took a few bits.'

'The omen was right then. Spooky!' said Mole. 'Joe stood on Mrs Bunion's roof and she got burgled.'

'Shut up about omens. And anyway, if the omen was right, it was because Joe made it right. Remember when he came out of her window and onto her roof? He had something in his beak. Well, *he* must be the burglar. And there's things missing from other houses.'

Mole stroked the short dark feathers on the side of Joe's head. 'Wow, a real thief.'

'Anyway, it's only a matter of time before everyone puts two and two together, specially if he's helped himself to some of Becky's earrings. When they find out, they'll make us get rid of him or put him in a cage. Bird prison. Like Alcatraz.'

'That was the Bird*man*'s prison,' said Mole. 'Right. Here's what we'll do. We'll find all the stuff and return it to everyone, then they might forget all about it.' That's what I like about Mole, she's always got a plan.

'Where d'you think he's hidden it?' I said. 'Tell you what, you search all the places he likes in your house, and I'll search in mine. See you tomorrow.'

I went home and started with Joe's Kleenex box. There were loads of greyish shredded tissues, a few fluffy

feathers and that bird tabley smell I
told you about earlier. I reached into
the corner, just more shredded tissue.
Except this was a greenish colour. And
on one piece you could just make out
the tip of the Queen's nose. This
wasn't shredded tissue, it was
shredded five pound notes! Talk about
feathering your nest. Joe appeared at
my side; he looked decidedly miffed.
He took hold of the paper and pulled
it back into his house. Now who's the
burglar, he seemed to say. Well, that
explained the missing milk money.
But no sign of any jewellery.

In the living room, everyone was
back in front of the TV. I checked the
corner of the mantelpiece where Joe
often sat and felt along the top of the
shelves. Nothing.

'What *are* you doing?' said Dad. I'd
made the mistake of walking in front
of the TV. 'You've not been hiding

stolen goods have you?'

'Course not,' I said. 'It's just a splurt alert, nothing else.'

'Well, you'd better get the dish cloth, hadn't you?' said Mum.

Chapter 8

'Find it, Joe. You've found it before,
find it again.'

It was the day after the policeman's
visit. Joe and I were out in the road
looking for the Emerald and waiting
for Mole. I hadn't managed to find
any missing jewellery – not a dickie
bird.

'Find!' Joe flew off as a police car
came up the road towards us and
stopped outside Mrs Bunion's house.
As the policeman knocked at her door,
I scrambled towards the house,

keeping my head below the hedge.
'Get over here, boy!' You had to hand
it to Mrs Bunion, nothing got past her.
Not me anyway.

'What is it?' I walked over to them,
squeezing past the ladder by the front
door. Well, I wasn't going to walk
under it, was I? Joe flew down and
landed on my shoulder.

'Get that thing away from here,' said
Mrs Bunion, jabbing a finger at him.

'Make your mind up, you just told
me to come over,' I said.

'I didn't tell you to bring that flea-
ridden bird with you.'

'Joe doesn't have fleas. And nor do I
now he's pecked them off. My patent
nit collector. He'll do your hair if you
want. You only have to ask.'

The bunion glasses misted over and
Mrs B went into orbit. The policeman
decided to step in before he found
himself at the scene of another crime.

'Now, now,' he said. 'Mrs Bunyan seems to think that you and Brown Mole know something about these burglaries.'

'Mole Black,' I said.

'Well, do you?'

'Of course not.' I decided attack was the best form of defence. 'If anyone's a criminal round here, it's her. Blinds drawn down on her windows all the time. Bet she's an international cactus smuggler or something.'

I stepped back to point up at the cactuses on the balcony and clipped the ladder with my toe. Honest, I barely touched it, but it slipped across the roof a few feet sending tiles and other bits slithering down and clattering to the ground. They missed the policeman by a whisker. I looked at him, was he about to arrest me for attempted murder? But he was just staring at the ground where the tiles had fallen.

'Well, well, well, what have we here then?' I swear he really did say that. They must teach it to them in police training college. Anyway, there on the ground amongst the shattered tiles was a pearl necklace, a watch chain, earrings, two gold bracelets, and some coins.

'My pearls!' said Mrs Bunion.

'Yes, Mrs Bunyan,' said the policeman slowly. 'I thought they might be. And I think I might know who some of the other stuff belongs to.'

'I can explain,' I began. I had one hand clamped round Joe's body to stop him going after the jewellery.

'Oh, I don't think there'll be any need for that,' said the policeman.

'Honestly,' I said, 'It's quite . . .'
'It's not you I want to hear from. It's Mrs Bunyan.'

'Me?' said Mrs Bunion, 'Why on

earth?'

'What exactly were Mrs Broomfield's watch chain and Mrs White's bracelets doing on your roof? You've been up your ladder quite a lot recently by all accounts. I'm not one to beat about the bush, Mrs Bunyan. It seems to me you've been paying a few visits to your neighbours' houses with the help of this ladder of yours. Then you've been secreting the ill-gotten gains on your roof. Am I right?'

I was squeezing Joe really tight, one false hop towards the jewellery and I knew we would've had it.

'Don't be ridiculous. My pearls were up there too,' said Mrs Bunion. 'Why would I put my own pearls up there?'

'Presumably to put us off the scent,' said the policeman. 'No, it's a clear-cut case, Mrs Bunyan, wasting police time by mounting a fake crime just to cover up your own villainous activities.'

'How dare you!' said Mrs Bunion. 'I shall be speaking to your superior officers.'

'Fine by me, you'll have plenty of time to do that at the station. Right now you can get in the car if you don't mind, while I finish off a couple of things here.'

The policeman took Mrs Bunion's arm and marched her over to the car. He opened the door and bundled her inside, just as Mole came up the path.

'What's going on?' she said.

'They've arrested Mrs Bunion for the burglaries.'

'Mrs *Bunion*?' said Mole.

'Keep your voice down,' I hissed. Then, loudly, for the benefit of the policeman, I said, 'Yes, Mole, everybody's stuff was hidden under a tile on her roof. She must've faked the burglary at her house. Isn't it terrible to think we've been living opposite a real criminal, disguised as a little old lady?' I glared at Mole to stop her asking any more questions. The policeman slammed the car door on Mrs Bunion and came over to us.

'I'll just bag up the jewellery and we'll be off.'

'Aren't you going to caution her?' I said.

'There'll be plenty of time for all that.'

'Pity,' I said.

'Here, lend us a hand with this stuff. Pick it up using the bag, don't touch it with your fingers, we don't want your prints on it. Forensics will be testing it. That's the way we'll prove it's Mrs Bunyan. Her finger prints'll be all over the stuff. Now, stay here a minute, you two, and keep an eye on things.' The policeman pointed at the bag of jewellery. 'I just need to go into the house and make sure it's all locked up. We don't want another burglary, do we?'

The policeman disappeared inside.

'That'll teach her,' I said.

'Er– Rob,' said Mole, 'I think we have a problem.'

'Rubbish,' I said, 'We've just got rid of a problem.'

'It's the finger prints,' and she pointed at Joe's claws.

'It's Mrs Bunion who should be worrying about fingerprints,' I said.

'Come on, Rob, think about it. They'll be checking for *fingerprints*.' Mole was using her *'I'm trying to be very patient'* voice on me, and it was getting on my nerves.

'Yes, so what?'

'Well, they're not gonna find any, are they? Or have you managed to forget who the real burglar was? They'll not find Mrs Bunion's finger prints – well, at least only on her own stuff. But what they will find on everything is beak prints and the odd claw print. They'll know it's Joe.'

'But how?' I said.

'Forensic testing and everything. They'll know it's a bird.'

'But they can't prove it was Joe that *took* the stuff. He could've found it on the roof. It's just, what's that word they use in *The Bill*, circumstantial evidence.'

'What if they go back into all the houses and do some more checks? He's bound to have left some evidence behind – a grey splurt here, a feather there. What are you going to do, whip round the street on a "splurt alert" with your dishcloth?'

'Well, what do you suggest? If they find out he's the burglar he'll definitely be taken away.'

'There's only one thing for it,' said Mole. 'We've got to get Joe to touch the stuff now in front of the policeman, then that'll explain why there'll be evidence of Joe in the tests.' Mole was obviously in her element. First she comes up with the terrible problem, then she finds the perfect solution. Meanwhile I'm left standing there waiting to be told what to do.

'OK,' I said. 'Let's get on with it. Shouldn't be too difficult. Joe can't take his eyes off the jewellery anyway.'

I took hold of the plastic bag, peeled it open, knelt down and slid the contents on to the ground. Joe leaned right forward on Mole's shoulder, ducking and tilting his head to get a better view.

'Oh dear,' said Mole very loudly for the benefit of the policeman. 'Idiot, Rob, now look what you've done.'

Joe hopped to the ground one foot away from the trinkets.

'Bother,' I said, as the policeman shut Mrs Bunion's front door behind him.

'Er, we're sorry, officer,' said Mole,
'But Rob's just dropped the stuff on
the floor and we've had a bit of
trouble keeping the bird off it. Don't
worry, we haven't touched it ourselves,
I'll just use my handkerchief to get it
back in the bag.'

'Blessed kids,' said the policeman. 'I
can't leave you for two minutes. Get
that bird out of here.' He took his cap

off and flapped it at Joe. Joe panicked, darted forward, seized Mrs Bunion's pearls and flew up with them. He circled the road before landing on Mole's roof.

'Damn!' said the policeman.

'Don't worry,' said Mole. 'I'll get them back.'

'Yes,' I said, 'Leave it to us, sir. You take Mrs Bunion to the police station and we'll collect the evidence. After all, it's not the most important bit is it, Mrs Bunion's own necklace? We'll call you when we get it. Don't worry, we'll keep it to ourselves.'

The policeman didn't have much choice. How was he going to tell his bosses that he'd left two children in charge of stolen goods? It wouldn't look good. And he couldn't go searching for the necklace now, or Mrs Bunion would smell a rat. Of course Mrs Bunion was a rat, but that didn't mean she couldn't smell another one.

'Ring me as soon as you find it. And wear gloves to pick it up.' As if to prove his point the policeman poked me hard in the chest. Then he grabbed the bag of jewellery out of my hand and walked back to the car.

'Phew! That was a lucky escape,' said Mole. 'I bet I know what Joe's doing up there. He'll be putting the necklace into another treasure hoard. See the way he's pushing at the tiles. Blimey, Rob, he's probably been storing stolen goods on all our roofs! What did your mum say about sticking with hamsters?'

'Better get up there and get it back,' I said.

Chapter 9

Climbing onto Mole's roof wasn't as
easy as you might think. We didn't like
to borrow Mrs Bunion's ladder – after
all you never knew whether they were
planning to fingerprint that, too – and
hers was the only one long enough to
reach right up past the gutter. In the
end we decided to scramble out of
Mole's bedroom window and onto the
roof that way. Mole went first, I
followed. The roof was sloping at
about 50 degrees and we had to
shuffle up a few feet to reach the

chimneys where it felt a bit safer. I'd
never had much of a head for heights.
I went on the London Eye once and
spent the whole ride lying on the floor
with a coat over my head.

Joe looked very surprised to see us.
Or maybe he was just flabbergasted by
the fuss we'd made getting up there.
All that puffing and panting and stuff,
why hadn't we just flown? We edged
up next to him and he hopped onto
my hand. He didn't mind us
pretending to be birds. I wondered for
an instant about that omen thing.
Would a flock made up of two kids
and a jackdaw perched on a roof bring
good fortune? Or did it have to be all
jackdaws?

'Where's he put the necklace then?'
said Mole. 'Ah, there it is.' You could
just see the pearls sticking out from
under a loose tile about a metre away.
Mole edged towards it.

'Careful! This roof's really slippery.'
'I'm fine. Oh no! Look at that!' Mole had knocked the tile out of the way, revealing not only Mrs Bunion's necklace but other jewellery too. She raised both hands in the air and turned towards to me. And then everything seemed to happen in slow motion. Her foot lost its hold, I reached out to grab her and got a handful of fresh air as she slipped down to the edge of the roof, hung for a second and then disappeared. There was a rustle and a dull thud as she hit the ground.

'Mole! Mole!' My scream sent Joe into a frenzy. He shot up into the air, and down the chimney. I stared after him. Mole's words echoed in my mind. 'A jackdaw flying down the chimney means death in the household.'

Numbly I eased myself over towards Joe's hoard and stuffed the bits in the pocket of my fleece. Then I shouted as loudly as I could.

Within minutes, there were people everywhere. Firemen to get me down from the roof, ambulance men at Mole's side. She looked more like a real mole than ever, wrapped tightly in a dark blanket with just her hands and face sticking out. Adults were shouting questions at me and all I could think was, what if I've killed Mole? Even if she'd chosen to ignore the jackdaw jinx, I shouldn't have. And anyway, it was me that had decided to keep Joe. Mole was going to die and it was all my fault.

Mum and Dad took me back home, they were looking very pale and talking at me all the time. I couldn't answer. I grabbed an old wooden pencil and shoved it inside my shirt against my skin. If I touched wood for long enough, would Mole be saved?

After about an hour, that policeman came to the front door. He'd obviously come to arrest me and I knew I deserved it. He was wearing his helmet, and in all this mess I found myself worrying about how he'd get in and out of the car.

'I'm glad you're here,' said Mum, bringing him into the front room, 'Maybe you can get some sense out of him. Really, I don't know what they thought they were doing.' She glared at me. 'Aren't you and Mole old enough to have stopped playing silly games?'

I looked at the policeman, expecting him to be angry. But his face was very calm and very serious. It could only mean one thing, Mole was dead.

'Leave him be, Mrs Mills. I'll talk to him.'

'I'll be in the kitchen if you need me.'

'What's happened to Mole?' I said,

as soon as Mum had gone out. 'Please tell me. Is she dead?'

'No, son, she's going to be OK. She was lucky, something must've broken her fall. She's got a nasty fracture in her arm, but otherwise they say she'll be fine.'

'Are you sure?' I felt like you do when you get the first lungful of fresh air after swimming underwater for too long.

'Yes. That's what the doctor said.'

'I thought she would die, when Joe flew down the chimney . . .'

'She'll be back home tomorrow.'

'I've got Mrs Bunion's pearls, they're still in my pocket, we managed to get them off the roof.'

'I'll take them.'

I felt in my pocket and pulled the necklace out. But it was tangled up in the other jewellery from the roof. I tried stuffing it all back in, but the policeman had spotted it.

'Just put it out on the table, son.'

'I didn't steal it. I'm not the thief.'

'You'll have trouble proving that won't you? Your fingerprints are all over it.'

'But it must have been Mrs Bunion.'

'Come on, Rob,' said the policeman. 'This is all a bit of a mess isn't it? Soon as you start covering things up you end up in worse trouble. I'm as guilty of that as you are. I should never have left you and Mole with the bag of stolen goods. Then you wouldn't have tipped the stuff on the ground to protect Joe. He is the burglar, isn't he?'

'Joe? He never . . .'

'Look Rob, Mole's fallen off the roof, Mrs Bunyan's arrested for something she didn't do. You can't go on protecting that bird forever can you?'

'How did you find out? Did Mole tell you?'

'D'you think she would?'

'No.'

'Well you're right about something then. It all came out at Mrs Bunyan's interview. She decided it was time to tell us the whole truth. See, she knew your bird was storing stolen stuff on her roof and on other roofs too. She'd been spying on the bird from her balcony. But she wasn't satisfied with getting the jackdaw into trouble. She was after you two, just waiting for the right moment to pin the burglaries on you. Apparently, you and Mole are a couple of delinquents who deserve what's coming to you.'

'What? She was setting us up? The mean, spiky . . .'
'Well, it's no worse than what you did is it? Letting me arrest her for something she never did?' I suppose he had a point.

'What's going to happen next?' I said.

'We've got to get all the jewellery back to your neighbours.'

'Do we have to tell them what really happened? That it was Joe?'

'I'm afraid we do. Like I said, you've

got to come clean. Face the consequences. I already have. Just look at me wearing this daft helmet. Back on foot patrol, aren't I, just because I made the mistake of leaving you and Mole with the jewellery. If your bird's a thief, you'll have to get rid of him – unless you're prepared to put him in a cage.'

'A cage? Joe can't go in a cage. He'd hate it.'

'Then find somewhere else for him. A long way from here.'

Chapter 10

That night I lay awake for ages. It's not easy to get to sleep with the point of a pencil sticking into your chest every time you move. When I finally dropped off, I had the strangest dream. One minute I was watching helplessly as Mole fell down the chimney, then she faded out and Joe appeared. Except it wasn't Joe at all, it was Mrs Bunion, dead in a field of cactuses. By morning I was totally exhausted. I felt terrified of going downstairs in case Mole had had a relapse overnight and the jackdaw jinx had come true after all. When I finally walked into the kitchen my heart missed a beat. Mum was sitting at the kitchen table, head in her hands.

'We've lost, Rob,' she said.

'Lost . . . who?' I whispered.

'Lost the dump.'

'Oh. But what about Mole?'

'She's fine.'

My knees gave way and I flopped down at the table. Dizzy with relief, it was a few moments before I could focus on what Mum had said. Then I felt guilty. In all the trouble with Mrs Bunion and the burglaries, I'd almost forgotten about the dump. In fact, since I'd had Joe, I hadn't been up there as much as before. It was as if I'd taken the best thing from the dump and then abandoned it. 'What's happened about the dump?'

'The appeal's failed, that's what,' said

Mum, 'The bulldozers are moving in. Short of lying down in front of them, we'll not stop them now.'

'Maybe we could persuade Mrs Bunion to lie down in front of them,' I said.

'I know the common's in a mess,' said Mum, 'and they're probably right when they say it's dangerous, but we could've cleared it up a bit and at least it was somewhere for you kids to go. Get you out from under our feet for a bit. I don't know, things round here seem to be going from bad to worse.'

Even Joe could sense something was wrong. Putting his head on one side he peered down at Mum. After that terrible start – and give or take some broken ornaments, splurted magazines and pecked ear lobes – they'd got quite fond of each other. He used to meet Mum on the way home from the shops and eat blueberry muffins on her shoulder. Now he flew down and wiped his beak gently on the sleeve of her jumper.

'Least we've still got you,' she said, stroking Joe's feathers. I didn't like to ask her for how long. 'Ugh! Splurt alert, Rob.'

About mid-morning I saw Mole's car backing into their drive. I gave them a few minutes, then Joe and I went round to see Mole. I just had to know she really was OK. Sitting on the sofa in their front room, she looked paler and smaller than ever, but she perked up when Joe started nibbling her plastered arm. Maybe he preferred it to her real arm, more branch-like.

'Am I glad to see you,' I said. 'I thought you were going to die.'

'So did I,' said Mole. 'Specially when I was hanging from the edge of the roof.'

'Like when Gandalf slips off that cliff

in the *Lord
of the Rings*.'

'Well almost,' said
Mole, 'but luckily for me
there was no fiery cavern
below. Just a sycamore bush.'

'I was so scared. You see, just as you
fell, Joe flew down your chimney and
well, you know what that means.'

'You don't still believe all that stuff
do you?' said Mole. 'Anyway, it's
impossible.'

'What d'you mean?'

'He couldn't have gone down our chimney. I told you before, it's got a grating on it. He probably just flew behind it or something.'

'Oh.' I must admit I felt pretty stupid, specially since I'd just wasted a whole night on horrible chimney dreams. How was I s'posed to remember about a manky grating? That was it, I was finished with jinxes and omens for good. No more touching wood. I reached inside my shirt, pulled out the pencil and laid it quickly on the table. But I couldn't resist giving it a quick stroke to thank it for anything it might have done to help Mole.

I told Mole everything the policeman had said, ending up with the bit about putting Joe in a cage.

'We can't do that.'

'I know,' I said. 'But we may not have a choice, unless we get rid of him.'

'We need a plan. Let's go and find the Emerald. I should be able to walk that far.'

Now who d'you think was the first person we saw when we got out into the street? Mrs Bunion, that's who, fizzing and hissing towards us. It was like watching a lit fuse sparking its way over to a stack of explosives – us! The first word we heard was 'DISGRACE', then I think it was 'ABOMINABLE, APPALLING', closely followed by 'DELINQUENT, NASTY', and 'PARENTS'. Maybe she was saying that her parents had been delinquents and that's why she'd turned out as nasty as she had. But I don't think so. Joe took one look at her and fled to the safety of the beech tree above our heads.

'Don't think I'll forget this! I can't get rid of you – much as I'd like to. But I can get rid of that bird.' Mrs

Bunion waved an arm towards Joe, and, good on him, a grey splurt hit the ground right at her feet.

'Bit to the right, Joe, and you'll get her next time,' said Mole. She didn't usually talk like that in front of Mrs Bunion, maybe the polite bit of her brain had got damaged in the fall.

'When I've finished,' said Mrs Bunion, 'everyone round here will know that thing's the culprit, I'll make sure of that. Either you get rid if it yourselves by this afternoon, or I'll do it for you.'

Joe had flown down into the middle of the road and was pecking at the Emerald. Mrs Bunion rushed at him, flapping her arms like a gigantic crow. Then she stopped suddenly, stared at the road and turned on her heel. 'Just get that thing out of here.'

We grabbed Joe and went back to Mole's house. I felt sick. Mrs Bunion

was mad, totally mad. I couldn't see any way out. The policeman, Mrs Bunion, the message was the same. I glanced at Mole, surely she'd come up with something? But she looked exhausted.

'Bunion's won, Rob,' she said. 'Joe'll have to go.'

'There must be another way,' I said. 'Here, Joe, get under my fleece so no one sees you.'

I don't think I've ever felt so bad. I couldn't stand the idea of losing him, specially when he was starting to fit in a bit better at home. Since she'd chucked Mick, Becky had hardly complained about Joe at all. And a couple of days ago I'd actually caught Gran trying to teach him to say *Pretty Polly*. That's Joe, I mean, not Mick. I wandered out into the street. Joe was struggling under my fleece so I lifted the hem slightly – and he was off. Up and away towards the dump. So much for keeping an eye on him.

Chapter 11

You know the phrase 'down in the dumps'? Mum had it on one of her posters. Well, I'd never really understood it. My dump was a place that made you happy, a 'land of opportunities' as Dad says. But as I clambered over the rubbish that afternoon, I knew exactly what it meant. Everything had gone wrong. I climbed past a pile of old boxes and broken bins right onto the very top of the heap, all the time whistling and calling for Joe. Why had he chosen to

go back up to the dump just then?
Had he guessed we meant to get rid of
him and decided to head home of his
own accord? Not that the dump would
be much of a home if it was packed
with offices.

I peered up into the trees as I had on
that first day when I'd been searching
for Joe's parents. No sign of him.
There was one strange thing though:
as I was looking around in the scrubby
bushes at the back, I caught sight of
Mrs Bunion walking back towards the
road. She didn't often come up here,
I hoped she hadn't come after Joe.

Flopping down on the edge of the
bath, I had an idea. You remember
how he enjoyed knocking the lids off
the coffee pots, especially when he was
bored or upset? Maybe that would
work now. There were a few old bowls
and a couple of cracked beer mugs in
the rubble next to the bath. I placed

them carefully along the rim, with
pieces of bark balanced across them.
Then I sat back and closed my eyes.

Less than thirty seconds later, there
was a rush of air and Joe came
swooping down. I didn't look at him.
I didn't say anything, I just carried on
doing my impression of Gran having a
nap after a good bird-free Sunday
lunch. Joe was in no mood to let me
rest, he hadn't forgiven me for

crushing him under my fleece. I opened one eye as he headed for the first bowl. He swiped at it sideways with his beak and sent the bark sliding down into the bath. Then he glanced at me, sidestepped past the second one and began on the third. And so on down the line. I waited until he had reached the end of the row and stretched out my hand.

'Come on Joe,' I said. 'Friends again.'

He stepped back a pace, tilted his head on one side and glared at me.

'I came to find you,' I said. 'Find . . . you.'

The word *find* had an instant effect. He darted up and swooped round and round above my head and disappeared behind the bath. Seconds later he was back on my shoulder with something in his beak. It was a piece of green stripy glass. I recognised it straight away.

'Wow, Joe, another Emerald! Where did you find it?'

He was off again, then back with another piece, and another. You could slot two of them together, like one of those 3D jigsaws.

'Let's go and look for the real Emerald, Joe. It must be part of the same thing.'

We headed over to the street.

'Find!' I said. Joe skirted round and came to rest beside a small hole in the road. He looked up at me. The Emerald had gone. Mole must have taken it. But why? She shouldn't have touched it, not without asking me. I ran over to her house.

'Why did you take the Emerald?' I said as she opened the door.

'What?'

'Why did you move the Emerald?'

'I didn't. It's still there.'

'No, it's not. There's just a hole.'

'Come off it Rob, it must be there. You're just having trouble finding it.'

'It's definitely gone. Joe found these other bits of glass at the dump, we were going to see if they matched our Emerald, but it's vanished.'

Mole looked at the pieces in my hand. 'Cool,' she said.

We went out to the road and I showed her the tiny hole. Now we were up close, we could see scratches on the surface around it where someone had levered the Emerald out of the concrete.

'Mrs Bunion,' said Mole.

'What?'

'I bet she took it. Remember how she stopped and stared at the road. She must've seen the Emerald, waited until we'd gone and come back for it.'

'Why would she do that? Why would anyone do that?'

'Because it's worth something. It

might be a real emerald.'

'Get a grip, Mole, it's just a bit of an old wine bottle.'

'Well, I'm going to find out,' said Mole. 'She'll have taken it back to her house won't she? What are we waiting for?'

'Armed reinforcements,' I said.

'There's no way I'm going anywhere near her house. Specially not with Joe. Just how hard did you bang your head when you fell off that roof?'

'It's up to you.' And she was off, running bent double like they do in war films when they're launching an attack. Joe and I had no choice really. We had to go after her.

'Are you mad?' I said as we crouched beneath Mrs Bunion's front window. 'You haven't even checked to see if she's in.'

'She is,' said Mole. 'Look.' I peered through the blinds. I could just make

out Mrs Bunion. She was filling a
watering can in the kitchen at the back
of the house. Laid out on the living
room table a couple of metres from
where we stood were pot-loads of
manky cactuses. Sitting next to the
cactuses, was the Emerald. But it

wasn't the only one. Set in a circle around it just like Stonehenge, were six or seven other pieces of glass all with the same stripy pattern.

'She's got loads of them,' Mole whispered.

'I saw her at the dump earlier, she's obviously been collecting them. Bet they're worth a fortune.'

'And we've just helped her find another piece.'

Uh-oh, we should have known better. It was that word again. *Find*. There was a flurry of wings. Joe rocketed up to the roof. A moment later he had disappeared down the chimney.

'Forget death in the family,' I said. 'It'll be death to Joe if she catches him. Whose bright idea was it to come back here?'

A couple of seconds later, Joe appeared on Mrs Bunion's table. I tapped the window softly. Mrs Bunion

was still in the kitchen. But how long
would it be before she came back
through?

'She's gonna get him,' I said. 'What's
that rhyme about four and twenty
jackdaws baked in a pie?'

'Blackbirds,' said Mole.

'I don't s'pose she's fussy which.'

'I can't bear to look,' said Mole, jumping from one foot to the other. Meanwhile Joe sidestepped past the cactuses and was calmly drinking from the nearest flower pot, stretching his neck up to let the water trickle down his throat. He looked as if he hadn't a care in the world.

'Doesn't he know he's playing with fire? Joe,' I whispered into the windowpane, 'get back out here. Quick before she *finds* you.'

Finds did its magic again. Joe hopped over, picked up our Emerald from the centre of the circle and flew back up the chimney. I thought of the time I'd tried to draw a circle round the stone and it had 'escaped', just as Joe had helped it to escape this time. Mole and I ducked to the side as Mrs Bunyan walked back into the room with a dustpan and brush. She stopped in front of the table and looked at the pieces of glass. Would she notice the Emerald had gone? Obviously not. With a flick of her wrist, she swept the pieces straight into the dustpan. Then she went back out into the kitchen and tipped them into the bin.

'Scram!' said Mole.

We fled back to the street as Joe came swooping down and landed on my shoulder. Mole took the Emerald from him and slipped it into the pocket of her jeans.

'So much for it being valuable,' I said. 'She'd hardly stick the pieces in the bin if they were worth anything.'

'Doesn't make any sense though does it?' said Mole. 'Why did she bother to dig it out of the road in the first place? She must've done it to spite us. She probably saw us playing with it and decided to take it away.'

'What a loser!'

Mole's mum came into the street and called her in. I wandered back home. It felt like another wasted afternoon. All that time worrying about Mrs Bunion when we should have been working on a plan to save Joe. Time was running out.

Chapter 12

Mum was sitting at the kitchen table colouring in another poster. This one was aimed fairly and squarely at the builders.

USE YOUR COMMON SENSE!
BACK OFF!

'Don't say a word,' she said. 'I know it's all a waste of time. But I've got to do something. Anyway we need to talk. I've had that policeman on the phone asking what we plan to do about Joe. Mrs Bunion's obviously been stirring things up. It's not going to work is it? We'll never keep Joe out of people's houses. And if we can't stop him, he'll have to go.'

'I'll keep a closer eye on him, I promise. Make him stay in more.'

'But he's used to coming and going as he pleases. Take that away from him and you might as well stick him in one of these.' She pointed across the room. On the floor next to the table was a golden budgerigar cage, fitted with curtains, swings and what looked suspiciously like a padded sofa.

'Gran brought it round,' said Mum. 'Kind of her really. It's her Joey's holiday home and she's done it up specially for our Joe. New curtains and everything. There's even a little picture of Gran on the mantelpiece next to the lucky horseshoe.'

Joe jumped down from my shoulder

and walked wide-eyed up to the shiny cage. It must've looked like one giant piece of jewellery to him; I bet he was wondering how he could lever it up into one of his rooftop treasure stores. I opened the door for him.

'Wanna look round, Joe?' He jumped onto my shoulder. 'Go on, try it.' With an angry flap, Joe retreated to his Kleenex box on the shelf. 'Guess he's voted with his wings.'

'Who could blame him?' said Mum. 'We all know it wouldn't be right to shut him up.'

'I could train him better. He's such a quick learner. He found the Emerald in the road, and lots more at the dump.' I emptied my pockets onto the kitchen table.

'What on earth . . . *Where* did you get this stuff? Looks like you've raided the bottle bank! You'd better get rid of it before you cut yourself.'

There was a knock at the back door. It was Mole. I could tell something was up.

'Rob, can you come out for a bit?'

'Shouldn't you be resting, Mole dear?' said Mum.

'I'm fine,' said Mole. 'Oh and Rob, bring those with you,' she said, pointing at the glass on the table.

'I've been checking some things out,' said Mole, as we reached the road. 'I looked up the local museums on the internet. And I think this glass might be ancient after all. Saxon or something.'

'Is that before or after King Henry VIII?'

'Before, idiot. Even more before than we are after.'

'But if it was worth something, why did Mrs Bunion chuck it away?'

'Well that's just it. D'you remember what you said about Joe being rare and how that could save the dump?'

'But he's not rare. He's common –
like the dump!'

'Very funny. But don't you see, it's
the same with the pottery. What if the
dump's an old burial ground or
something?'

'Spooky.'

'Spooky or not, they couldn't build
on it, at least not straight away. And
that would explain why Mrs Bunion
binned the glass.'

'Why? She's the last person to be
spooked by a burial ground.'

'Because,' said Mole, going all patient
on me again, 'she'd stand to lose
money, that's why. If the offices don't
go ahead, she won't sell her land and
she loses out. Big time.'

'So you think she knows the site's
important but she's destroying the
evidence?'

'Which explains why she wants us to

keep away from the dump. In case we find something.'

'And why she hates a bird that likes shiny things.'

'*She* might hate him but I bet any sensible archaeologist would love him. Who's been the best at finding the glass? You? Me? No way. We can hardly find the Emerald even though it's been stuck in the same bit of concrete for years. No, it's all down to Joe. If he can help people dig the site and find the relics, then no one will want to get rid of him. And apart from Mrs Spiky Bunion, the neighbours don't want these offices, so they'll be grateful to Joe too.'

'It's like the jackdaw jinx in reverse,' I said. 'We find Joe, get to the truth about the Emerald and the dump is saved. So he turned out to be a good omen after all.'

'I thought you'd dropped the omen

stuff. You might as well say the dump's got special powers because it sent Joe to save itself.'

My head was beginning to ache. It was all getting a bit too deep for me.

'Whatever. What do we do now?' I said. 'No time to lose, the bulldozers are on their way.'

'We ring the police,' said Mole. 'Well, you do anyway. You're the one that watches *The Bill* all the time.'

It took a while to get through to our policeman and when we did he wasn't exactly pleased to hear from us.

'What did you say?' he spluttered. 'You're asking me to go into Mrs Bunyan's house and rifle through her rubbish sacks? They might've put me back on the streets but they haven't got me emptying bins yet.'

'She's throwing away valuable stuff,' I said. 'National treasure. There must be a law against it. On *The Bill* last week they . . .'

'Shut up! I've been on late shifts and I haven't seen that episode yet. Why can't you just leave Mrs Bunyan alone? What's she ever done to you? Apart from trying to get you arrested for burglary of course.'

'She's taking the dump away.'

'Good thing too. Refuge for down-and-outs and thugs.'

'It's not. It's full of lots of good stuff.'

'If you're wrong about this,' said the policeman, 'you're in trouble. I'll get you for wasting police time.'

Twenty minutes later, Mole and I were lying in wait for the police in Mole's front garden. We were keeping an eye on Mrs Bunion's house too: we didn't want her doing a runner.

'Shhh!' said Mole from the crow's nest in the sycamore bush. 'I thought I heard a siren.'

'They should be here by now,' I said.

'It's my turn to be look-out. You might hurt your arm again.'

'They're probably getting a team together to do a raid,' said Mole. 'After all, Mrs B might turn nasty, set one of her spiky cactuses loose on them.'

'Or bombard them with bunions from her supercharged specs. Or nobble them with the watering can.'

'Shhh. That was definitely a siren wasn't it? Oh no! I can't believe it. It's squeaky brakes. That policeman's only coming along the road on a bike.' Mole was right. And it wasn't any ordinary bike. It looked like it had come straight off my dump. All rusty and bent. So, no sirens, no flashing lights, just him, a wrecked bike and a pair of rubber gloves.

'D'you want some help?' I asked, as he wobbled to a standstill outside Mrs Bunion's. 'Back-up, that's what they call it isn't it? Just in case she makes a

run for it.'

'Yes, you can help. You can help by making yourselves scarce.'

'Oh.' All that stuff they're always telling us at school about being helpful to policemen and we get landed with PC Stresshead.

He left his bike against the wall and knocked on Mrs Bunion's door. It took her a long time to answer it. She was probably far too busy destroying national treasures in a back room. Our policeman followed her inside.

'Come on, let's go and watch,' said Mole jumping down from the tree. By this time peering through the blinds into Mrs Bunion's front room was second nature to us. We got there in time to see our policeman emerging rubber-gloved from the kitchen with several pieces of stripy glass. He was holding them at arm's-length. Tomato soup was dripping from his gloves onto the carpet. At least I think it was tomato soup – but of course it could've been blood. If we put our ears to the windowpane, we could just make out what they were saying.

'Well, Mrs Bunyan, what's this stuff doing in your bin?'

Mrs Bunion frowned and shrugged her shoulders. No prizes for guessing what she said next. 'Never seen them before in my life, officer.'

'Bet she'll claim they've been planted on her,' said Mole. 'Get it? Planted – like all her cactuses . . .'

Mrs Bunion walked away from the table towards the door. The policeman was obviously in no hurry to arrest her. He wasn't even looking at her, he was busy examining the emeralds. Now Mrs Bunion had picked up a large trowel from the other end of the table and she was creeping very slowly towards him.

'I think you're in a spot of bother,' said the policeman, with his back to her. At the word *spot*, Joe was up, away, and down that chimney like a flash. Then, as Mrs Bunion lifted the trowel high above the policeman's head, Joe flew at her, piercing one of the red spots on her glasses. It was like watching a giant black dart torpedoing straight at the bull's eye. She howled with rage as the blow glanced off the plastic and cut into her nose. The trowel fell to the floor and the policeman wheeled round.

'*Spot of bother!*' I laughed. 'That's what Dad used to say when he attacked Becky's boyfriend's pimple. Joe must have thought it was an order.'

'Hang on a minute, you saying your Dad attacked Mick's pimple?'

'No, Joe did. Just think, if Joe hadn't gone for Mrs Bunion's stupid spotty glasses, that policeman would've had a bad case of trowel-head. It could've been *murder.*'

The policeman was on the radio calling for back-up – shame he hadn't listened to me in the first place – and Mrs Bunion was handcuffed to the table leg. Soon there were squad cars

everywhere and our spiky neighbour
was being bundled into a car.

'Yes!' shouted Mole, punching the air
with her fist as the cars disappeared
round the bend in the road. Then,
'Ouch!'

'Word of advice, Mole, if you're gonna
do that, don't use your broken arm.'

Chapter 13

And that was the last we saw of Mrs Bunyan. The last anybody at Win Hill saw of her. A month later her house was up for sale and two lorries arrived to take away her belongings. One lorry for the cactuses and the other for the rest of the stuff. It turned out that Mrs Bunyan was very big in cactuses. A worldwide expert actually. She'd got herself into debt buying more and more rare specimens and that was why she needed to sell the land. I know it's a strange thing to say after all that had happened, but Mole and I felt rather sorry for her and we decided that from that moment on she deserved to be spelt properly. That's Bunyan like the man who wrote the famous story, not Bunion like the corns on Gran's foot. When we thought about it, we could sort of understand that if Mrs B had spent loads of money importing rare cactuses from Australia, she wouldn't really have wanted a jackdaw pecking them to pieces.

But to be honest, the sudden disappearance of Mrs Bunyan was the last thing on our minds over the next few months. Things were really on the move at Win Hill. You see Mole was right. The Emerald turned out to be a piece of an ancient glass beaker and the dump was a small Saxon burial ground. I must admit I didn't even know they made glass in Saxon times. Apparently only a really important person would've had a beaker like that, so, even though the Emerald wasn't a real emerald, it was still pretty valuable. And of course it was quite right that all this should've been found on my dump – since beaker and burial both begin with 'b'.

Within a few weeks of Mrs Bunyan going, loads of archaeologists with shaggy beards moved onto the site. Must admit, this was a bit of a mixed blessing. It meant that the dump was saved, which was fantastic, but it also meant that it wasn't really a proper dump any more, because the first thing they did was to remove the junk. The holey buckets, the buckled bikes, everything had to go. And what with hoards of bearded archaeologists with trowels and suited project managers with clipboards and journalists with noisy mobiles and woolly volunteers with sandwich boxes, the end of our road was a bit like Piccadilly Circus.

The other amazing thing to tell you was about the TV. We were on it – live! It was only the local News, but everyone at school was dead impressed and if you ever want to see the DVD I'll lend it to you. The only bad part is when they call me *Robin* and make the usual joke about me and Joe being *birds* of a feather. And then there's the embarrassing bit when Dad walks right across in front of the camera, talking on his mobile to Craig from the office.

As for Joe, the hero of the story, the number one dump-saver, well, it was like Mole said, the neighbours were so grateful to him for stopping the offices that they decided he could stay. All the training we'd given Joe with the Emerald stood him in good stead and he was really helpful to everyone on the dig. He became a sort

of mascot for them. Mum said that they should re-name the dump *Joe's Common,* but someone pointed out that could be read the wrong way. I think Mum was just trying to re-use some of her slogans from the posters.

It's true that Joe didn't come up with the goods for the archaeologists every time. In fact he found far more rusty coke cans than Saxon relics and he once got terribly possessive about the silver foil on the site manager's sandwiches. But every now and then he would find something really good and that made up for the little bits of trouble he caused here and there – the missing pieces of thousand-year-old jewellery and the grey splurts all over the archaeologists' plans.

All the valuable remains from the burial site were put on display in the museum and they invited Mole and me down to a special preview to see

what they'd discovered so far. We
didn't take Joe with us in case he
wanted to 'borrow' any of it back.
They'd mostly found pots, but there
were a couple of iron spearheads and
some beads. Odd to think the beads
were over a thousand years old

because they looked pretty much like Becky's. They'd only managed to piece together one glass beaker from the site and, as we peered in at the museum display, we could see there was still a little bit missing from the rim. We were just turning to leave when Mole slapped her pocket.

'Oh no,' she whispered.

'What's wrong?' I said, 'That's our beaker.'

'The Emerald,' said Mole, 'It's still in my pocket. Quick, come outside.' She virtually pushed me out of the museum door and round the corner of the building. Then she sat down right there on the pavement and began emptying her pockets. About half an hour later – well, she did have a lot of stuff in there – she pulled out the Emerald. It had been in her pocket ever since Joe had taken it from Mrs Bunyan's table.

'Come on, Rob,' Mole was saying, sucking her finger where it had caught on the edge of the glass. 'We'll have to give it back to them. Fancy me having it all that time without even knowing.'

Now this is where you might go off me a bit. I expect you've been thinking I'm a pretty good person up until now. The sort of person that takes in baby birds, helps to save dumps and uncovers archaeological sites. Well I am. And what I said next surprised even me.

'Let's keep it.'

'What?' said Mole.

'We could put it back in the road.'

'But we can't,' said Mole. 'It's the final piece of the beaker. And the beaker's really special, everyone should see it.'

'But if it hadn't been for us they'd never have found any of it. We should be allowed to keep just one bit. The Emerald's always been in our road.'

'Take this and you'll be a thief. Worse than Joe.'

'But it's our Emerald. I don't believe in omens any more, but the Emerald's special. It shouldn't be shut away in a display case. It should be free. It'll escape anyway.'

'*What?*' said Mole. 'Are you totally mad?'

'It's escaped before. I never told you, but one night I put a chalk ring on the concrete round the Emerald so I'd be the first to find it in the morning, and, you're not going to believe this, but the Emerald escaped!'

Mole stared at me. I could tell she was impressed. This was my moment of glory, I finally knew something she didn't.

'Really? You sure?' said Mole.

''Course. The chalk circle was still there, but the Emerald was way outside it.'

'Wow!' Mole peered closely at the Emerald. 'There's just one thing. You don't suppose someone else could have redrawn the line, do you? Like me, for instance. To get you back for being such a *CHEAT!*'

Typical! All those years believing in the Emerald's special disappearing powers only to find it had been down to Mole. And then she had the cheek to call *me* the cheat! Mole and I marched back into the museum in silence. We handed over the Emerald to the curator without even looking at each other. Now museum curators aren't exactly famed for getting excited about things, but we knew we'd done something special when he stroked his beard and said very quietly, 'Well I never' – *twice!*

We watched as the curator opened the display cabinet up and very carefully slotted our Emerald into the rim of the green beaker. A perfect fit. The dump had come up with the goods just when it really mattered. It was like I said before. Sometimes you just got a bit of glass, sometimes a beaker with a hole in it and very rarely a whole beaker, just like this. Mole punched the air – she didn't use her broken arm this time – and we went home to find Joe. But he wasn't there.

Chapter 14

Joe had vanished. Honestly – I'm not just inventing this bit so the story doesn't finish on Chapter 13. Although, what with jinxes and omens and Grans who throw salt over their shoulders, I wouldn't want to take unnecessary risks. No, Joe had definitely gone. After all we'd done to help him to stay with us, he'd decided to leave without a word – or a squawk.

'Bet it was something to do with the glass beaker,' I said a few days later as Mole and me circled the dump for the hundredth time whistling and shouting for him. Not that he had much chance of hearing us with that JCB thundering up and down.

'What d'you mean?'
'Well, once the glass beaker was complete and the dump was saved he must have felt his job was done. Or maybe he got really angry because you gave the Emerald back to the museum.'
'So it's my fault now is it? Get real, Rob. He's a jackdaw, he doesn't know anything about the beaker, or about

saving dumps. OK, so he went after the Emerald and stuff, but he was just doing what jackdaws do best – thieving.'

'But how come he disappeared on the exact day we gave the Emerald back?'

'Ever heard of coincidence?'

'Yes but . . .'

'Hey, you two!' It was the site manager. 'Come over here a minute.' We waded through six tons of mud towards the JCB. 'Have you found Joe yet? One of the volunteers said he saw him last week with another bird.'

'But Joe never has anything to do with other birds,' I said. 'Unless you count torturing sparrows on the bird table.'

'Apparently,' said the site manager, 'he was picking at a piece of silver foil when another bird just like him came down and joined in. They had a quick tug of war with the foil and flew off together.'

'So that's it,' said Mole. 'He's found a friend.'

'A girlfriend probably. Just like you, eh?' The site manager winked at me and nodded towards Mole.

'Grow up!' said Mole. I couldn't have put it better myself. We turned our backs on him and struggled back through the mud.

'So that's how Joe repays us for looking after him,' I said. 'He takes off with the first bird that comes along. Maybe we should've kept him inside.'

'I can't believe you said that. We always agreed he would never be shut in. The best thing about having him was that he chose to be with us.'

'I'm just going to miss him, that's all.'

But I needn't have worried. Two weeks after he was spotted with his new friend Joe reappeared in the Kleenex box. Maybe the two of them had had a row over something and he

needed some space to think. And that's more or less the way things have stayed. Sometimes we don't see him for weeks, sometimes he drops in and out every five minutes just like old times. I have to admit that Joe's new regime, as Mum calls it, has taken a bit of getting used to. Part of me still wants him to be around all the time like a normal pet, but deep down I know it's better this way. I'm still waiting for him to bring his new friends home to meet us. They can sit on our roof and earn us a fortune.